Dragon Danger

Written by Cynthia Rider,
based on the original characters
created by Roderick Hunt and Alex Brychta
Illustrated by Alex Brychta

OXFORD
UNIVERSITY PRESS

Floppy was dreaming about
dragons.

Floppy saw a baby dragon with
its mother.

6

The mother dragon saw Floppy.

"Go away," she roared.

The dragon roared again and
flapped her wings.

She flew at Floppy.

"Oh help!" he said.

WHOOSH! Flames came out
of the dragon's mouth.

Floppy hid, but the
dragon saw him.

Floppy ran onto a bridge.
WHOOSH! Flames came
out of the dragon's mouth again.

"Help!" said Floppy.
"The bridge is on fire."

13

Floppy ran back across
the bridge.

He ran past a rock and saw the
baby dragon again.

The mother dragon roared at
Floppy. She flew up onto a
high rock.

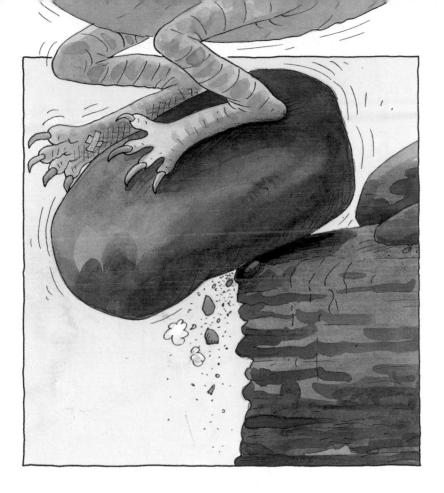

Oh no! The rock started to fall.

CRASH! The rock fell
down . . .

but Floppy pulled the baby
dragon out of danger.
"Phew! Just in time," he said.

What a brave dog!

Talk about the story

Why did the mother dragon roar at Floppy?

Why couldn't Floppy hide from the dragon?

How do you think Floppy felt when the rock started to fall?

What other dragon stories do you know?

A maze

Help Floppy find his way out of the dragon's maze.